Puffin Books

WILLIE WHISKERS

When other young mice are doing their sums, Willie Whiskers is dreaming – of ice-cream, of cake, of chocolate, of anything, in fact, to fill his ever-rumbling tummy. Keeping his tummy satisfied has become a full-time job for Willie, who is always slipping off to the larder, and into trouble.

Dad has his toe bitten, Jenny has her party ruined and Henry finds something very peculiar in his school custard, but somehow Willie always escapes safely back home, none the worse for his adventures. But he's getting fatter all the time, and the mousehole isn't getting any bigger!

Margaret Gordon trained as an artist at Camberwell and St Martin's School of Art in London, and spent some years teaching. She illustrated many books, including the original Womble stories. *Wilberforce Goes on a Picnic* (a picture book) was the first of several books she wrote and illustrated herself. She died in 1990.

Also by Margaret Gordon

HELP!

Picture Books

Willie Whiskers

Margaret Gordon

PUFFIN BOOKS

PUFFIN BOOKS

Published by the Penguin Group
Penguin Books Ltd, 27 Wrights Lane, London W8 5TZ, England
Viking Penguin, a division of Penguin Books USA Inc.
375 Hudson Street, New York, New York 10014, USA
Penguin Books Australia Ltd, Ringwood, Victoria, Australia
Penguin Books Canada Ltd, 2801 John Street, Markham, Ontario, Canada L3R 1B4
Penguin Books (NZ) Ltd, 182–190 Wairau Road, Auckland 10, New Zealand

Penguin Books Ltd, Registered Offices: Harmondsworth, Middlesex, England

First published by Viking Kestrel 1989
Published in Puffin Books 1991
10 9 8 7 6 5 4 3 2 1

Text and illustrations copyright © Margaret Gordon, 1989
All rights reserved

Printed in England by Clays Ltd, St Ives plc
Filmset in Times (Linotron 202) by
Rowland Phototypesetting (London) Ltd

Contents

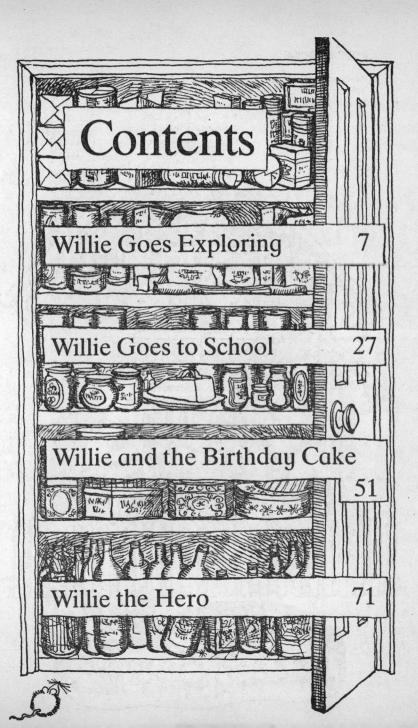

Willie Goes Exploring

Mum and Dad and Jenny and
Henry lived at 3, Orange-
blossom Avenue. Henry was
eight and had a pet mouse. It
lived in a cage in his bedroom.
Jenny was five. She didn't have
a pet mouse but she would have
liked one.

Willie Whiskers lived at 3, Orangeblossom Avenue. His front door was a little hole in the skirting board of the kitchen. His back door led to the larder. This was the most important part of the house for Willie Whiskers and his family. It was full of good things to eat.

Willie Whiskers lived with his mum and dad, Mr and Mrs Whiskers, and all his brothers and sisters. There were lots of brothers and sisters. Willie Whiskers wasn't sure how many. Some days he thought there were nine and some days he thought there were ten.

Willie Whiskers couldn't

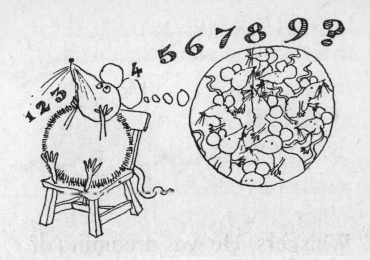

count very well. He was also
bad at adding up. He was best
at eating up. He was fat. He
was very fat. He looked like a
hairy golf ball.

"A young mouse should not
be so round," said Mr
Whiskers.

"What?" said Willie

Whiskers. He was dreaming of biscuit crumbs.

"You're too fat," said Mrs Whiskers. "If you're not careful, you'll get stuck one day."

Every morning the little mice had lessons. One day, Mr Whiskers decided to teach them how to add up.

"Now, sit down all of you

and we'll do some addition,"
he said.

"What?" said Willie
Whiskers. He was dreaming of
spilt ice-cream.

"Adding up," said Mrs Whiskers.

They all sat down like good little mice and did their sums. All, that is, except Willie Whiskers. Pictures started to float through his mind. 2 gingernuts + 3 chocolate biscuits + 7 chocolate-chip cookies ... Willie felt quite faint. "I must be empty," he thought.

He put down his paper and pencil, and slipped away through the back door and along a short passage to the larder. Mr and Mrs Whiskers had made a tiny hole that led into the larder. Willie Whiskers rarely used this hole. It took so long when all his family was there. It didn't seem sensible to

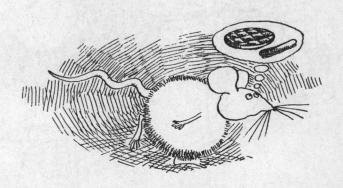

be queuing when he could be
eating. Willie had made his own
little hole. No one else knew
about it. It was round the back

and up the side, and came out
on the top shelf.

The top shelf was the biscuit
shelf. Willie Whiskers

spent many happy after-
noons up there among the
cream crackers and the

chocolate fingers, when he
should have been doing his
lessons.

Today his shelf was full.
"Someone's been shopping,"
he said.

"I'll have a nibble of this," he said to a packet of custard creams. "I'll have a bite of this," he said to a box of shortbread.

Willie Whiskers felt better. "I'll just have a look at the lower shelves," he decided.

He missed his footing and bounced right down to the bottom shelf, where there were dark-green, cobwebby bottles. They had labels that said things like gin and whisky and brandy.

"Bother," he said. He was
too tired to climb up.

"Stale biscuits," he muttered.
He squeezed under the larder

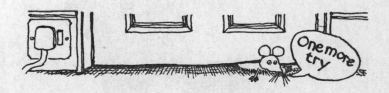

One more try

door. No one was about. There
was a trail of toast crumbs
which Willie cleared up as he
went. The trail led into the

sitting-room, and was joined
by some biscuit crumbs that
were scattered all round Dad's
armchair. Willie Whiskers
tidied those up as well.

He suddenly felt very sleepy. His eyes started to shut. He saw a pair of slippers in the corner.

fluffy lining

He crept into the left one. It was soft and warm and fluffy. The very thing. He went straight to sleep.

Mum came home. Henry came home. Jenny came home. Mum put Dad's slippers to warm by the fire.

Dad came home. He was cross. He had had to wait ages for a bus. He saw the slippers and he felt better. He put on the right one. Lovely. He put on the left one. Struggle, push,

struggle. He couldn't get his
foot in.

Willie Whiskers dreamt that a
hippopotamus was sitting on
him. He was getting flatter and
flatter and . . . He woke up. He
sank his teeth into Dad's toe.

"OUCH!" exclaimed Dad.
He flung the slipper into the air
and hopped up and down on
one leg.

"Henry, if you let that mouse
out again," said Dad, "it's
going back to the pet shop."

"But, Dad..." said Henry.

Willie Whiskers tumbled out of the slipper and made a dash for the mousehole. He was so flattened he got in quite easily.

"Where have you been?" asked Mrs Whiskers.

"You haven't done your addition," said Mr Whiskers.

"What?" said Willie.

"Adding up," said Mrs Whiskers.

Willie Goes to School

Willie Whiskers and his nine, or
was it ten, brothers and sisters
were doing take away sums.
Willie tried hard, but a noise
somewhere between his toes
and his ears interrupted him. It

was that tummy of his. It was
rumbling again.

"Mustn't let it disturb
anyone," he thought. "Better
top it up a bit."

He put down his paper and

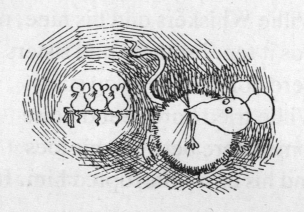

pencil very quietly and crept out into the passage. Once out of sight, he scampered along to his hole in the larder wall. He climbed up and hopped in.

The larder looked a bit empty. "Stale biscuits," he muttered. "Someone needs to do some shopping."

He took a rice-crispie and put it back. He wanted something more interesting. A little treat

to help him forget his take away sums. A breeze wafted past his nostrils. His nose twitched. His whiskers shook. There was a lovely smell. He had to follow it.

He climbed down to the shelf
that was filled with the dark-
green, cobwebby bottles. He
squeezed under the larder door,
ran across the kitchen and
found himself in the hall. He
followed his nose. He

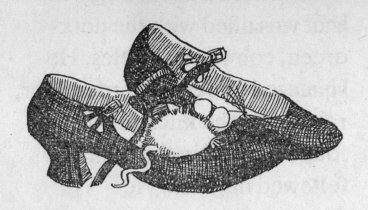

clambered over some shoes,
and found a row of coats and
hats and jackets all hanging up
together. He sniffed Dad's
jacket. Tobacco and beer. He
sniffed Mum's coat. Mothballs.
Just a minute; Henry's jacket.

"Here we are," thought
Willie.

Willie Whiskers hopped into
the first pocket. No. Second.

No. Third. Yes. There it was – a
half-eaten bar of chocolate with
a squidgy peppermint centre.
He didn't even have to open it.

"I'll have that," he said.

Some time later, Willie's
tummy rumble had quite
disappeared. So had the
chocolate. He settled down for
a little snooze under the bits of

string, chewing-gum wrappers and crumpled tissues in the corner of Henry's pocket. No one would find him there. He

didn't really want to go home until the take away sums were over.

It was time for Henry to go to school.

"Work hard," said Mum.

"Yes, Mum," said Henry.

"And don't take your mouse to school," said Dad.

"No, Dad," said Henry.
He grabbed his jacket and
ran out of the house.

Willie Whiskers dreamt he was
in a big sailing ship. He sailed

into a storm. The wind blew hard and the waves got bigger. The boat was going up and down, up and down.

After register, teacher showed the children how to do take away sums. Henry felt in his pocket. He was sure he'd left half a bar of chocolate there to help him with his sums. All he

could find among the string,
tissues and fluff was a
minced-up wrapper. He didn't
find the chocolate and he didn't
find Willie.

Willie Whiskers slept on in
Henry's untidy pocket. He
dreamt that the storm was over
and the ship had dropped
anchor by an island covered in
chocolate-bar trees. He swam
ashore and ran across the warm

sand. He was just about to pick a pawful of chocolate bars when he woke up. He peeped out of Henry's pocket.

"And then you carry one," said the teacher.

"Oh, horrors. Not take away sums," thought Willie. "They seem to be everywhere."

His nostrils twitched and his whiskers trembled. A lovely smell wafted past his nose. The

I don't believe it

chocolate bar in his tummy had
sunk down. He was beginning
to feel empty again.

He crept out of Henry's
pocket and ran across lots of
pairs of knees. Some were
warm and some were cold.
Some were clean and some
were dirty.

"Miss!"

"Miss! There's a . . ."

"Miss!"

"Miss! I've just seen a . . ."

Willie Whiskers squeezed under the classroom door and scuttled along the corridor. He ran over the headmaster's shiny

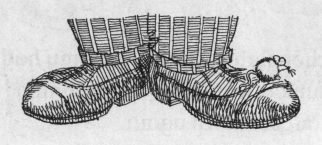

shoes and round the secretary's high-heels, and all the time the wonderful smell grew stronger. It was an exciting mix of stew and custard and baked beans and treacle, mixed up with a few other things.

He stopped. He sniffed.

There it was – the school
kitchen. Big, big saucepans of

stew and cabbage and mashed
potato and rice pudding and
peas and prunes and carrots
and other treats. He tried to
keep calm. He'd never seen
so much food before. Why
bother with a larder? He'd
often heard Henry and Jenny

talk about school dinners.

"Yuk," said Henry.

"Yuk, yuk," said Jenny.

Willie didn't think it was yuk at all. It was lovely.

"I'll have a bit of this," he said to the stew, "and a bit of that," he said to the rice

pudding. "And a mouthful of these," he said to some bright-

green peas, "and a nibble of
that," he said to an enormous
pan of cauliflower cheese with
crispy bits round the edge.
When he was full up, he nestled
down among a pile of warm
oven gloves.

He woke with a jolt. The
kitchen was full of people

clattering plates and spoons and rushing around with trays and pans.

Willie Whiskers was startled. He climbed over a knobbly trayful of hot sausages. He tripped and landed on a gigantic iced sponge and skidded straight into an

enormous pan of warm, yellow custard.

"Ooh, lovely," cried Willie Whiskers.

A large lady with a large
ladle scooped him up with a
helping of custard, and plonked
him into a dish already
occupied by a piece of iced
sponge. She handed the dish to
a small boy wearing a familiar
jacket.

"Thanks," said Henry.
Henry walked slowly to his

table. His custard seemed
rather lively and his sponge
cake was swimming towards
him. It had two bright little eyes.

"A mouse," he whispered, "a
mouse in my custard." Henry

couldn't believe his luck. He
scooped Willie out and popped
him in his pocket.

Willie Whiskers cleaned his
fur. The custard was delicious.

"Very warm." He shut one
eye.

"Very comfortable." He
dozed off.

After school Henry went home.
He opened the front door. He
was going to sneeze. He
reached for his hanky and

pulled out Willie Whiskers
instead.

Henry sneezed.

"Ugh, uggh, ugggh," said
Willie. He ran as fast as he

could to his mousehole.

"Wherever have you been?" asked Mrs Whiskers.

"I suppose you got stuck somewhere," said Mr Whiskers. "You haven't done your subtraction."

"My what?" said Willie Whiskers.

"Taking away," said Mrs Whiskers.

Willie and the Birthday Cake

Willie Whiskers and his brothers and sisters were learning "How to Escape from Cats". Willie had to be the cat for this lesson. He liked

jumping out on his brothers and sisters and giving them a fright, but after a while he got bored. While they were searching for new hiding-places, he crept out

of the room, along the passage and round to his hole in the larder wall.

Inside, the larder looked different. There were lots of new, interesting-looking

packets on his biscuit shelf. He
climbed down a shelf.
Everything looked much
prettier than usual.

There was a stripy jelly,
plates of sandwiches, bowls of
crisps and peanuts. There were

little chocolate cakes, bigger
cherry cakes and one enormous
cake on a stand. It was so

beautiful, it took Willie Whiskers' breath away.

It had thick pink icing all over and a row of little white sugar flowers round the edge. There was a white satin ribbon tied round the side and six pink candles in the middle. Around the candles it said Happy Birthday Jenny in white icing.

Willie was overcome. He just stood quietly in the middle of all those lovely things and looked at them.

Then he said, "I'll have a bit of that," to a plate of cheese sandwiches. "I'll have some of

that," he said to the bowls of crisps and peanuts.

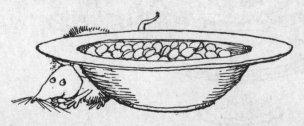

Then his throat felt a bit scratchy, so "I'll have a bite of that," he said to the plate of stripy jelly.

Willie Whiskers was beginning to get full, so he thought he'd miss out the

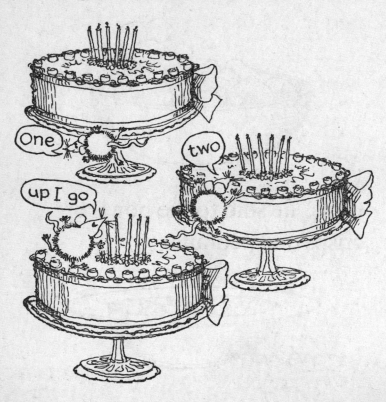

chocolate and cherry cakes. He
grasped the edge of the cake-
stand, gave three big swings
and was up beside the pink
icing, the white ribbon and the
sugar flowers.

He didn't know where to
begin. He didn't want to spoil
the cake.

"I'll just have that," he said
to a sugar flower.

He climbed up on to the top
of the cake and sniffed at the

words Happy Birthday Jenny.

"Um, butter icing," sniffed Willie. "I'll just have a little bit." He ate the H from Happy.

"I'll just have a little bit more," he said, and ate the ny at the end of Jenny.

He meant to stop but it tasted

I wish I could spell

so good. Perhaps he'd better have some of the middle word just to even it up.

"That's enough," he said. He

didn't want to spoil the pattern.

Willie Whiskers was very full now. "I'll just put my feet up for a second," he murmured.

He burrowed into the side of the cake and curled up in the soft light sponge.

"I'll go home soon," he said,
and went to sleep.

"I don't want her to come to my
party," said Jenny.

I hate her

"You must invite her. She's
your cousin," said Mum.
Cousin Clarinda had blue

eyes and yellow curls and was
good at lessons. She was
terrified of mice.

Cousin Clarinda came to the
party. She came in a blue, frilly

dress, which was the same
colour as her eyes. She had lots
of blue ribbons in her yellow
hair. She looked lovely.

"Isn't she a picture?" said Aunt Mavis.

"That dress matches her eyes," said Aunt Matilda.

"And so well behaved," said Aunt Muriel.

"I'm not going to like this party," thought Jenny.

Henry offered to bring down

his pet mouse to give Cousin
Clarinda a fright.

"If you do, you'll get no
birthday cake," said Mum.

"If you do, that mouse goes
straight back to the pet shop,"
said Dad.

So Henry didn't.

They played several games.
Cousin Clarinda won all of

them. Then they went into the kitchen for tea. Mum hadn't brought the cake in yet. She was keeping it as a surprise. No one noticed the little nibbled bits in the sandwiches or the holes in the jelly. Everyone was getting full. Some of the naughtier girls were starting to flick peanuts at each other. Henry joined in. Clarinda didn't. Mum decided it was time

3. **4.**

to bring in the cake.

"Oh no!" said Mum.

"Oh no!" said Dad.

"Oh no!" said Jenny.

On top of the cake it said
appy day Jen.

"I knew they couldn't spell at
that shop," said Dad.

"Cut the cake, birthday girl,"
said Mum.

Jenny decided she must be
nice to Cousin Clarinda. She cut

the first piece especially large
and gave it to Clarinda.

Clarinda didn't have time to say
thank you. A small, furry ball
rolled out of the cake, off the
plate, across the table and
bounced into Clarinda's lap.

Clarinda gave a piercing shriek
and fainted. Clarinda
hit the floor.

Which way to the mousehole?

So did Willie Whiskers. He
scampered across Clarinda's
frilly blue skirts, got caught
in her yellow hair, got tied up
in her ribbons, and then made
a dash for the mousehole.

"Where have you been?"
asked Mrs Whiskers.
"I'm not sure," said Willie.

Willie the Hero

Mum had gone to work. Henry had gone to school. Jenny had gone to school. Dad was in a hurry to get to work. He drank his tea and rinsed his cup. He grabbed his jacket and ran out

to catch the bus. He had left the kitchen tap on.

Mrs Whiskers was giving everyone grooming lessons. How to arrange whiskers

neatly. How to wash properly behind the ears. How to keep a tail well scrubbed and neatly curled when not in use.

Willie Whiskers enjoyed
grooming lessons. Although he
knew he was a bit fat, he felt he
was a fine figure of a mouse. He

went to look at himself in the
mirror by the back door. As he
was so near the larder, he
thought he might as well check
the shelves.

There was a nice, moist,
crumbly apple pie with just a
slice missing. "I'll have some of
this," he said.

There was a lump of
cheese on a plate. "I'll have

a bit of that," he said.

He was beginning to get full.
He scuttled down to the
cobwebby shelf at the bottom of

the larder and rolled under the door.

Perhaps there was something nice to eat in the kitchen.

"Ah, the bread bin. Shut. Never mind." He squeezed his nose under the lid and levered it up. Wonderful. Brown bread, white bread and lots of convenient crumbs. "I'll tidy these up," he said.

He remembered Jenny's party. Surely there would be a few tasty bits and pieces on the floor? No. Someone had cleared up well. Anyway, the

floor looked funny. It was shiny. Wet. Yes, that was it. Wet. Very wet.

He heard a tinkly sound.
The tap was on. The sink was
full. Water was slopping

over the edge. Willie Whiskers
was full of apple pie, cheese and
breadcrumbs, but for once he
was wide awake. He slid down
the refrigerator flex and

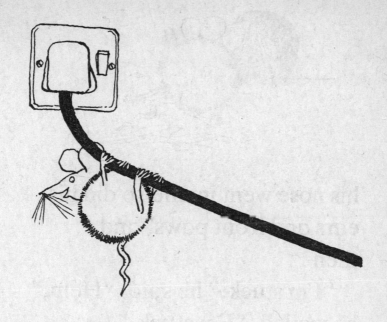

part running, part swimming,
got to the mousehole just before
the water. His whiskers went in,

his nose went in and so did his
ears and front paws, and
then . . .

"I'm stuck," he said. "Help,"
he wailed, "I'm stuck."

Too much apple pie, too
many breadcrumbs.

"Help," he yelled. "I can't come home." He started to cry.

Mum came running. "Why, Willie Whiskers," she said, "whatever is the matter? Why don't you stop crying and come right in?"

"Can't," sobbed Willie.

"Oh," said Mrs Whiskers, "I see. You're stuck!"

Mr Whiskers came running.

"If you can't come in, you'd better go out," he said.

Willie Whiskers did a little wriggle. Water started to slop in around him.

"Stop," said Mrs Whiskers. "What's happening?"

"There's a flood," said Willie. "That's why I came, I mean that's why I tried to come . . ."

He gave a little sob, "home."

"Stay there," said Mr
Whiskers.

"I'd rather not," said Willie.
"My bottom is cold and my tail
is freezing."

"Please," said Mrs Whiskers.

"Please," said all the nine,
or was it ten, brothers and
sisters. How could he say no?

Mrs Whiskers read him
stories about brave mice, and
Mr Whiskers tried again to
teach him take away sums,

although Willie would have preferred him not to. His brothers and sisters played sitting-still games with him like I Spy with my Little Eye, and

I Spy something beginning with W

combed his whiskers.

After a while, Willie
Whiskers noticed water oozing
in around him. He heard a

rumbling noise somewhere
around his middle.

"It's my tummy," he said,
"my tummy's going down. Fill
me up again or the water will
get in."

So all day Mr and Mrs
Whiskers and Willie's brothers

and sisters made a chain to
the larder and back. They

fed Willie with gingernuts and
apple pie and cheese. His

brothers and sisters moved so
quickly that Willie found
counting them even more

difficult than usual. He decided
there must be twelve of them.

Willie filled the hole
beautifully. No more drops of
water squeezed past his
middle.

"Willie Whiskers is a hero,"

said Mr Whiskers.

"Willie Whiskers is a hero,"
said Mrs Whiskers.

"Our Willie is a hero," said
all his brothers and sisters.

When Mum got back from
work, she waded into the
kitchen and turned off the tap.
It took a long time for the water

to go down. Just as the last of
the water drained away, and
Mum and Henry and Jenny and
Dad were mopping away in
their wellies, Jenny thought she
saw a small, brown, furry
bottom and little pink tail in the
skirting board. She watched it
give several wriggles and

disappear into a tiny hole in the
skirting.

For the rest of the day Willie
was a hero. It felt very nice. No
one did any lessons. They kept

saying "Thank you," and
bringing even more apple pie
and gingernuts. But for the first
and probably the last time in his
life, Willie Whiskers couldn't
eat another crumb.

Mr Whiskers even brought

him a tot of whisky from one of
the cobwebby bottles in the
bottom of the larder. He said he
had siphoned it off specially, to
warm up Willie Whiskers' tail.

Willie took a sip. He felt as if
he had drunk flames. His tail,
which had been a bluish-purple,
glowed pink. Mrs Whiskers
rubbed his fur down and gave
him two hot-water bottles.

"I'm a hero," said Willie
Whiskers. "I'm a hero because I
eat too much and because I'm

so fat," said Willie. "I must get fatter," he said, and fell fast asleep.

The End